Y0-CQO-848

★ *GREAT SPORTS TEAMS* ★

THE NEW YORK

BASKETBALL TEAM

Randy Schultz

Enslow Publishers, Inc.

40 Industrial Road   PO Box 38
Box 398   Aldershot
Berkeley Heights, NJ 07922 Hants GU12 6BP
USA   UK

http://www.enslow.com

WITHDRAWN

Library of Congress Cataloging-in-Publication Data

Schultz, Randy.
    The New York Knicks basketball team / Randy Schultz.
        p. cm. — (Great sports teams)
    Includes bibliographical references (p. 43) and index.
    Summary: Surveys the key personalities and some important moments in the history of the New York Knicks basketball team.
    ISBN 0-7660-1281-6
    1. New York Knickerbockers (Basketball team)—History—Juvenile literature. [1. New York Knickerbockers (Basketball team)—History. 2. Basketball—History.] I. Title. II. Series.
GV885.52.N4 S35   2000
796.323'64'097471—dc21
                                                                    99-053164

Printed in the United States of America

10 9 8 7 6 5 4 3 2 1

To Our Readers: All Internet addresses in this book were active and appropriate when we went to press. Any comments or suggestions can be sent by e-mail to Comments@enslow.com or to the address on the back cover.

Illustration Credits: AP / Wide World Photos.

Cover Illustration: AP / Wide World Photos.

Cover Description: Patrick Ewing.

CONTENTS

*K*nicks forward Dave DeBusschere slides over to guard Rick Barry of the Golden State Warriors. In the 1969–70 playoffs, DeBusschere averaged 16.1 points and 11.6 rebounds per game.

GREATEST MOMENT

An original member of the National Basketball Association (NBA), the Knicks had never won a league title in their twenty-three seasons of play. Fans hoped that 1969–70 would prove to be a different story.

Long Overdue

Led by center and captain Willis Reed, guard Walt "Clyde" Frazier, and forward Dave DeBusschere, the Knicks rolled to a league-best 60–22 record. Included was a then-record eighteen-game winning streak. The Knicks had an early record of 23–1.

"There was no go-to player," said DeBusschere. "Everybody (was) willing to take the big shot. It put a lot of stress on the defense."[1]

Could This Be Their Year?

In the first round of the playoffs, New York defeated the Baltimore Bullets in seven hard-fought contests.

That was followed by a second-round victory over the Milwaukee Bucks that New York wrapped up in just five games. All that stood between the Knicks and their first NBA championship was the Los Angeles Lakers.

The Lakers had three future Hall of Famers in their lineup, including center Wilt "The Stilt" Chamberlain, forward Elgin Baylor, and guard Jerry West.

The Captain

One thing was certain for the Knicks. They were going to depend on Reed—"The Cap'n," as his teammates called him—to lead them past the Lakers. And Reed would have his hands full against the veteran Chamberlain.

The best-of-seven championship series opened at Madison Square Garden. In Game 1, the Knicks, led by Reed's 37 points, got past Los Angeles, 124–113. But the Lakers evened things up in the series, winning Game 2, 105–103.

The next two contests were played in the Fabulous Forum in Los Angeles. Game 3 was a classic thriller. With just 3 seconds remaining in regulation time, DeBusschere hit a jump shot to give the Knicks a 102–100 lead. But West took a pass and fired a 65-foot shot that went in as the buzzer sounded. The Knicks managed to overcome the L.A. attack, winning in overtime, 111–108.

Game 4 was another overtime thriller. The Lakers won that contest, 121–115. The series was now even at two games apiece.

Reed Goes Down

Game 5 shifted back to the East Coast. With just 3:56 remaining in the first quarter and the Knicks trailing, 25–15, misfortune hit New York. While driving toward the basket against Chamberlain, Reed fell to the floor. He grabbed his left leg as he lay in pain.

Despite their misfortune, the Knicks seemed to gain momentum. The entire New York squad pulled together. They came from behind to defeat L.A., 107–100, to take the series lead, three games to two.

But without Reed in their lineup for Game 6 in Los Angeles, the Knicks seemed to lose the spirit that had carried them in the previous contest. New York lost to the Lakers, who were led by Chamberlain's 45-point effort, forcing a Game 7 back in New York.

Knicks stars of the 1970s. From left to right are Bill Bradley, Dave DeBusschere, Jerry Lucas, Willis Reed, Walt Frazier, Earl Monroe, and Dick Barnett.

"Willis was the captain," remarked Frazier. "He kept us together. Without him (Reed), I didn't think we could win it all."[2]

"Will Willis Play?"

Moments before Game 7 one player was missing from the Knicks lineup: Reed. "Coming back to Game 7 at the Garden, it was 'will Willis play?'" stated Knicks forward Bill Bradley. "That was the big question."[3]

Following their warm-ups and their return to the locker room, the Knicks came back to the floor to start the game without Reed. A capacity crowd of 19,763 fans strained to see if their fallen hero would play. The door to New York's locker room opened.

"I remember him (Reed) taking some treatment with the leg," said DeBusschere. "He was in the locker room. Just before we were to take the floor, I remember going over to him and saying, 'We only need you for a couple of minutes, big guy.'"[4]

The Leader Emerges

Walking slowly and deliberately, Reed entered the court as his teammates finished their warm-ups. Although he could barely run, Reed was determined to be in New York's starting lineup as the game began.

"This is what I dreamed about as a high school kid," remarked Reed. "This is what I had worked so hard for in college. And not only me, but everybody else in that locker room, that for me not to go out there, I would have been letting them [the team] down. I wouldn't let that happen."[5]

Willis Reed celebrates the Knicks first title. He was named NBA Finals Most Valuable Player.

With the capacity crowd roaring their approval, Reed lined up against Chamberlain. It did not take long for Reed to make an impact. He hit the first basket of the game from the top of the key. Moments later, while dragging his injured leg behind him, Reed again hit another jump shot, this one from twenty feet out.

That was all the Knicks needed, and all that the captain could give. He left the game and did not return.

Frazier totaled 36 points and 19 assists in leading the Knicks past the Lakers, 113–99, for the team's first NBA title.

Bill Bradley summed up what Reed did for the Knicks. Bradley said, "At that point the team had been lifted several levels of belief in themselves. It was like magic."[6]

*K*nicks guard Carl Braun defends against Bob Harrison of the Minneapolis Lakers. This game was played at the 69th Regiment Armory, the Knicks home before Madison Square Garden.

HISTORY OF THE KNICKS

The Knicks were not always on top of the world, as they were in 1970 when they won their first NBA championship. In fact, life for New York's pro basketball team was a bit humbling in the beginning.

The Early Days

The New York Knickerbockers began play in the Basketball Association of America (BAA), a forerunner of today's NBA. The first BAA game took place on November 6, 1946. The Knicks defeated the Toronto Huskies, 68–66, before a crowd of seven thousand fans in Toronto's Maple Leaf Gardens. Knicks guard Ossie Schechtman scored the first official points in BAA history.

"It was just a simple give-and-go," recalled Schechtman. "I made the first basket of the game. Nothing elaborate. Just a plain two-point basket."[1]

The 1946–47 Knicks would eventually finish the year with a record of 33–27. That was good for third place in the Eastern Division. Sonny Hertzberg was the team's leading scorer, averaging 8.7 points per game.

In their early days, the Knicks would play their home games either at the eighteen-thousand seat Madison Square Garden or in the 69th Regiment Armory, which seated only fifty-two hundred.

"Everything was a laugh," said Marty Glickman, former Knicks radio announcer. "Sure, they played hard and hated to lose, but we had fun."[2]

The BAA and the National Basketball League (NBL) merged to become the NBA in August 1947. That same year saw Carl Braun join the New York team, where he led the team in scoring and assists and was named the NBA Rookie of the Year.

New York continued to build, and as they entered the 1950s they got their first African-American player, Nat "Sweetwater" Clifton. The Knicks bought the six-foot seven-inch, 225-pound forward's contract from the Harlem Globetrotters.

Inside and Out

Another pair of players were added in the 1950s, Harry Gallatin and Dick McGuire. They quickly become known as Mr. Inside and Mr. Outside, respectively. Gallatin was known for his rebounding and inside scoring. McGuire was a guard who could shoot the ball from more of a distance.

The New York Knicks Basketball Team

Nat "Sweetwater" Clifton was the Knicks first African-American player, joining the team in 1950. He averaged 8.5 rebounds per game over his seven-year Knicks career.

Coming Close

By the 1952–53 season the Knicks had established themselves, winning the NBA's Eastern Division title. Unfortunately, New York lost to the Minneapolis Lakers, four games to one, in the NBA Finals.

That would be the closest New York would come to an NBA title in the 1950s. Between the 1959–60 and 1965–66 seasons, the Knicks continually finished last in the NBA's Eastern Division.

The Pieces of the Puzzle

In the mid-1960s the Knicks began to put together a team that would win the NBA title in 1970. The first part to that puzzle arrived in the 1964 NBA Draft in the form of a six-foot nine-inch center named Willis Reed.

History of the Knicks

Soon other pieces were added to the puzzle, including the likes of Cazzie Russell, Dave Stallworth, Bill Bradley, Dave DeBusschere, and Walt Frazier. Around Christmas 1967 a scout for the Knicks, Red Holzman, was promoted to head coach. A little more than two years later, the Knicks would be champs.

The nucleus of that Knicks championship team stayed intact. In 1973, New York, having added Earl "the Pearl" Monroe and Jerry Lucas, would once again be crowned NBA champs.

Some Tough Years

By the end of the 1973–74 season, Lucas, DeBusschere, and Reed had all retired. By the end of the 1976–77 campaign, Frazier had been traded and Bradley had retired. Their replacements could not help the Knicks rise back into championship form. Holzman soon retired as head coach.

Willis Reed returned to coach the Knicks, and in the 1977–78 season, he took the team to the playoffs. A year later, he was fired and replaced by Holzman.

Things did not get much better for the Knicks as they entered the 1980s. One highlight, however, came in 1984–85. That year, Bernard King led the league in scoring.

Hitting the Lottery

By the end of the 1984–85 season, though, the Knicks' fortunes finally began to change. That year, in the NBA's first-ever lottery draft, the luck of the draw

The New York Knicks Basketball Team

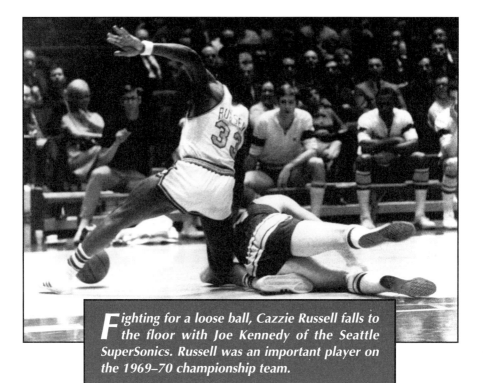

*F*ighting *for a loose ball, Cazzie Russell falls to the floor with Joe Kennedy of the Seattle SuperSonics. Russell was an important player on the 1969–70 championship team.*

gave New York the first choice. New York used it to select a franchise player—Patrick Ewing.

Ewing could not change the fortunes of the Knicks all by himself, and New York finished last again in 1985–86. Rick Pitino was hired as head coach for the 1987–88 campaign. Pitino installed an up-tempo game, and the Knicks began to win. Ewing was surrounded by talented players such as Mark Jackson, the 1988 NBA Rookie of the Year.

By the end of that season the Knicks had made it to the playoffs for the first time in four years, but lost in the first round. The team added Charles Oakley and rookie Rod Strickland to the lineup in 1988–89 and won the Atlantic Division title.

*W*alt "Clyde" Frazier drives to the basket against members of the San Diego Rockets.

GREATEST KNICKS PLAYERS

ive of the greatest players in New York Knicks history include Willis Reed, Walt Frazier, Dave DeBusschere, Earl Monroe, and Patrick Ewing. Each of these players either are, or will be, enshrined in the Naismith Memorial Basketball Hall of Fame. All five of these men were selected to the NBA 50th Anniversary All-Time Team.

Willis Reed

Willis Reed was selected by the Knicks as the team's top draft choice of 1964. That season, he averaged 19.5 points and 14.7 rebounds. For his efforts, he was named the 1965 NBA Rookie of the Year.

The 1969–70 campaign was considered Reed's finest. That season marked the first time in NBA history that a player was selected MVP for the season, the All-Star Game, and the finals in the same year. To top that off, the inspirational leader of the Knicks led his team to their first NBA title.

When he retired, Reed was the Knicks' career-rebound leader with 8,414. He had also scored 12,183 points for an average of 18.7 a game. He once scored 53 points in a game in 1967.

An eight-year Knicks captain, Reed was again chosen NBA Finals MVP in 1973 when the Knicks won their second NBA championship. "He is always their captain, a heroic figure in the classical sense," said Michael Burke, former president of the New York Knicks. "New Yorkers somehow learn that it was

Leaping into the air, Earl "The Pearl" Monroe shoots over Jo Jo White of the Celtics.

The New York Knicks Basketball Team

Willis, wounded as he was, who came off the trainer's table to win the championship in 1970."[1] In 1976, Reed was the first Knicks player to have his number, nineteen, retired.

Walt Frazier

Known to millions of Knicks fans as "Clyde," Walt Frazier was a first-round pick of New York in 1967. During his ten seasons in a Knicks uniform he was named to four All-NBA first teams and two second teams. He was an All-Defensive first team selection for seven straight years.

Frazier was a star on the New York championship teams in 1970 and 1973. In Game 7 of the 1970 NBA Finals, Clyde scored 36 points, added 19 assists, and grabbed 7 rebounds. Throughout his career, he averaged 18.9 points in 825 regular season contests, as well as 20.7 in ninety-three playoff games. His number, ten, was retired by the Knicks in 1979.

Frazier has worked for many years as a Knicks broadcaster. He is known for his enthusiasm and colorful commentary.

Dave DeBusschere

Forward Dave DeBusschere began his NBA career with the Detroit Pistons in 1962–63. This former No. 1 draft pick became the youngest player/coach in NBA history at age twenty-four. He held that position with the Pistons from 1964 to 1967.

DeBusschere was widely acclaimed as one of basketball's greatest defensive players. After being traded to the Knicks in 1969, he helped lead the team to two NBA titles in a four-year span.

"DeBusschere had a tremendous amount of knowledge of the game," said Reed. "We had a better ball-handling team because he could pass and make the play. He played to win and he understood how the game was played."[2]

In 1982, DeBusschere returned to the Knicks as general manager. The Knicks had already retired his number, twenty-two, in 1981.

Earl Monroe

Earl Monroe played for thirteen seasons in the NBA with the Baltimore Bullets and the New York Knicks. He was the second-overall pick by the Bullets in the 1967 NBA Draft. In 1968, he was named the league's Rookie of the Year.

The Pearl, as Monroe was known, was a member of the 1973 Knicks championship team. He was known for his ball-handling skills, acrobatic shots, and flashy style of play. "One of the things I learned early in my career, even in college, was how to play to the crowd," recalled Monroe. "And it became very important to me to have the crowd on my side because it just made my juices flow."[3]

Patrick Ewing

The New York Knicks selected Patrick Ewing as their first-overall pick in the 1985 NBA Draft. In his first fourteen seasons in a Knicks uniform, Ewing scored over 22,000 points and added over 10,000 rebounds,

Patrick Ewing shoots over Chris Mullin of the Indiana Pacers. In 1996, Ewing was named one of the fifty greatest players in NBA history.

setting team records in both. He is also the team's all-time leader in steals and blocked shots. The talented center earned NBA Rookie of the Year honors in 1986.

"The thing I like most about Patrick Ewing is his mental toughness," said former NBA star Nate Thurmond. "He comes out to win and to play hard every night."[4]

*N*ed Irish (second from the right) is shown here at a meeting to celebrate the addition of the Cleveland Cavaliers to the NBA. Irish helped found both the Knicks and the NBA itself.

GREATEST KNICKS COACHES

t has often been said that behind every good team there is a good coach and general manager. The Knicks have had several great coaches and general managers over the years.

Edward S. "Ned" Irish

Ned Irish was truly one of the founding fathers of the NBA. His efforts helped organize the league. He also helped form the New York Knicks, one of the league's original franchises.

In 1934, Irish became director of Madison Square Garden. One of his first event ideas was to hold college basketball double headers, an event that gained instant popularity. Known as The Boy Promoter, Irish also helped standardize the rules and coaching methods used in basketball.

Irish helped put together the first Knicks team, and he had his hand in everything—hiring the coach, signing the players, setting up the team's radio broadcasts, and promoting the club. "I had a great admiration for Ned Irish," said former Knicks player Sonny Hertzberg. "He quietly gave to charities, and he ran the Knicks first class."[1]

Irish was recognized for his efforts when he was elected to the Basketball Hall of Fame in 1964 as a contributor to the game.

Joe Lapchick

Long before the formation of the NBA, Joe Lapchick was playing professional basketball. In fact, he started his pro career at age seventeen. The money he made from playing basketball went to help his immigrant parents, who needed his support. For nineteen years, 1917 to 1936, he played for various teams that barnstormed across the United States. He was best known as the center for the legendary Original Celtics. Lapchick was considered by many at that time to be the game's first real pivot star.

He retired as a player in 1936 and became the head coach at St. John's University in Queens, a borough of New York City. Lapchick led St. John's to four NIT championships before moving on to the Knicks. He replaced the first Knicks head coach, Neil Cohalan, after the 1946–47 season. Lapchick was head coach of the Knicks for nine years, until the 1955–56 season.

Lapchick helped turn the Knicks around. He guided New York to the seventh game of the NBA Finals for two years running, 1951 and 1952. The Knicks lost to the Rochester Royals and Minneapolis Lakers, respectively.

In the 1952–53 season, the Knicks won the Eastern Division title, then lost to the Lakers, four games to one, in the 1953 NBA Finals.

Unfortunately, Lapchick could only do so much, and the Knicks began to slide. At the end of the 1955–56 season they finished last in the Eastern Division. Lapchick left the Knicks following that disappointing campaign. In 1966, he was elected to the Basketball Hall of Fame.

William "Red" Holzman

Red Holzman played for eight seasons in the NBA as a guard with the Rochester Royals, leading them to an NBA title in 1951.

Following his retirement as a player, Holzman landed a coaching job with the Milwaukee Hawks in 1954. He continued coaching the Hawks even after they moved to St. Louis. Midway through the 1956–57 season, however, Holzman was fired as coach.

Red Holzman joined the Knicks in 1959 as their chief scout. He did not return to the coaching ranks until December 1967, when he replaced the legendary Dick McGuire as the Knicks head coach. The team was in fifth place. By the end of that 1967–68 season, Holzman had New York winning and in third place. By 1970, the Knicks were champions.

Holzman is considered to be a coaching genius. He had the Knicks playing a conservative and defensive-minded game. "Red tries to give the impression that he's a hard, tough, impersonal coach," said Willis Reed during the Knicks 1970 championship run. "He's really

*J*oe Lapchick was head coach of the Knicks from 1947 to 1956. He led them to three Eastern Division titles.

just a pussycat, with more knowledge of basketball than any man I've ever known."[2]

The Knicks would win one more NBA title, this one in 1973, under his leadership. Holzman was soon looked upon as a legend in New York, as well as throughout the NBA.

Holzman was elected to the Hall of Fame in 1985. On March 10, 1990, the Knicks retired Holzman's number, 613, for the 613 wins he amassed in his fourteen seasons as New York's head coach. At the time of his death in 1998, he was the only Knicks head coach to ever be so honored.

*P*at Riley was the Knicks head coach from the 1991–92 season through the 1994–95 season. He led the Knicks to the 1994 NBA Finals, the team's first appearance since 1973.

Pat Riley

In Pat Riley's first season he established the Knicks as a physically dominating team. The team reached the second round of the playoffs, but lost in seven games to the eventual NBA-champion Chicago Bulls. It was the same story the following season. Once again, the Knicks lost to the Bulls in the playoffs.

Then, in 1993–94, New York made it to the NBA Finals for the first time since 1973. But a championship would elude them again, with the Houston Rockets foiling the Knicks this time.

*H*ead Coach William "Red" Holzman and team captain Willis Reed hold the 1970 championship trophy.

GREATEST KNICKS SEASONS

W hile Knicks' fans have experienced many great seasons throughout their team's history, no season shines more than the 1969–70 campaign.

1969-70

That particular season marked the team's twenty-fourth season in the NBA. At that point in time no franchise had ever waited longer to win an NBA title than New York. The Knicks dominated the regular season with a 60–22 record, tops in the NBA.

The campaign also saw New York win a then-record 18 straight games, including a last-minute, come-from-behind victory over the Cincinnati Royals that gave them the record-setting 18th win.

But the trail to the NBA championship was not an easy one for the Knicks. They played against Earl "The Pearl" Monroe and the Baltimore Bullets in the opening round. The first game went into overtime. The Knicks, by way of a clinching basket by Willis Reed with 31 seconds remaining, broke a 117–117 tie, and secured the win. The final score was 120–117.

Reed came through again in Game 5. He scored 36 points and pulled down an equal amount of rebounds. New York won, 101–80, breaking the series tie of two games apiece. The series went to a seventh game. His right knee aching, Reed again led the Knicks to victory, 127–114, ending the series.

Reed then led the Knicks past the Milwaukee Bucks in the second round. Facing rookie sensation Lew Alcindor (later known as Kareem Abdul-Jabbar), Reed played a very physical game, keeping the first-year player away from the basket. Reed led the Knicks past the Bucks in just five games.

It was then on to the championship round against Wilt Chamberlain and the Los Angeles Lakers. The emotional lift the Knicks got from the return of the injured Reed in Game 7 was more than the Lakers could handle. The Knicks crushed Los Angeles, 113–99, to win the NBA title in front of a home crowd at Madison Square Garden.

The 1972–73 Championship Season

The 1972–73 Knicks squad had finished in second place in the Atlantic Division. They were eleven games behind the front-running Boston Celtics; but the Knicks record was a bit deceptive.

Coach Red Holzman had played Reed sparingly throughout the regular season, trying to rest Reed's

The New York Knicks Basketball Team

injured knees as often as he could. Holzman wanted a healthy Reed ready to go for the playoffs that year.

The Knicks once again faced the Lakers in the NBA Finals. Los Angeles was the defending league champion. The Lakers won the opening game, 115–112. But it was all downhill for L.A. after that.

The Knicks came back from that first-game loss to win four straight games—and their second NBA title. Reed led the way for the Knicks in Games 3 and 4, scoring 21 points in each contest. He poured in 18 points in the fifth, and final, game of the series, won by New York, 102–93. For his efforts, Reed was voted MVP for the championship series.

Charles Oakley played the power forward position for New York from 1988 to 1998. He was an important part of the team that reached the 1994 NBA Finals.

"In the locker room after our second championship, as I looked around at my teammates I thought of how I liked something about each of them,"[1] said Bill Bradley.

1993–94

Pat Riley was at the helm of the Knicks for the 1993–94 season, and on the court Patrick Ewing led the team. During the regular season, New York had finished first in the Atlantic Division, with a record of 57–25. Ewing led the team in scoring and was second in rebounding to Charles Oakley.

Riley made sure that the Knicks were prepared for each contest. "He [Riley] screens hours upon hours of videotapes of the Knicks and their opponents—two or three times," said *Vanity Fair* writer Ken Auletta.[2]

In the opening round of the playoffs, the Knicks faced the New Jersey Nets. New York defeated its metropolitan rival, three games to one, in a best-of-five series.

New York faced the Michael Jordan-less Chicago Bulls in round two. In the deciding seventh contest in front of a sold-out Madison Square Garden crowd, the Knicks, led by Ewing's 18 points and 17 rebounds, beat the Bulls, 87–77. This ended Chicago's three-year reign as NBA champs.

The Knicks moved on to the 1994 Eastern Conference Finals and a matchup against the Indiana Pacers. Again New York would go to a seventh game before the series was decided. In that final game it was Ewing who scored the winning basket on a slam dunk to give the Knicks the victory, 91–90.

The New York Knicks Basketball Team

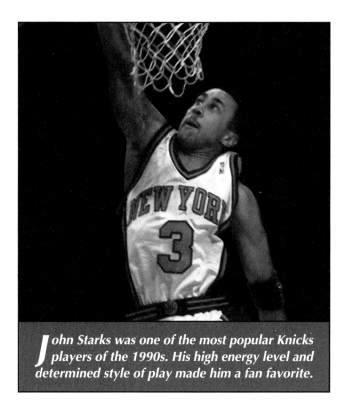

J ohn Starks was one of the most popular Knicks players of the 1990s. His high energy level and determined style of play made him a fan favorite.

The Finals

It was on to the 1994 NBA Finals against the Houston Rockets. Once again the Knicks were driven to a seven-game series.

Houston enjoyed a nine-point lead in Game 7, 72–63, with 9:18 remaining. But New York outscored Houston, 21–14, in the game's final nine minutes. With 2 seconds left and the Knicks trailing 86–84, John Starks missed a three-point jumper that would have given the Knicks the lead.

It was a disappointing end to what had been an exciting season. In the end, the Rockets won, 90–84. For the record, the Knicks played twenty-five playoff contests. No team had ever played in more. Unfortunately, New York fell one win short.

*J*eff Van Gundy gives instruction to players Larry Johnson (#2) and Marcus Camby. Van Gundy took over as Knicks head coach in March 1996, and led the team to the 1999 NBA Finals.

CINDERELLA SEASON

On the evening of June 17, 1999, Knicks forward Marcus Camby was supposed to be at a Macy's store in New York signing autographs for people purchasing men's cologne. That appearance was cancelled because Camby was doing something else that night: playing in the NBA Finals. It was something that nobody thought possible when the Knicks began the 1998–99 season.

Jeff Van Gundy

Following a path very similar to the one Red Holzman led, head coach Jeff Van Gundy guided the Knicks toward the twenty-first century.

Van Gundy joined the Knicks as an assistant coach on July 28, 1989. He held that position until he was named head coach of the Knicks on March 8, 1996, replacing Don Nelson.

Under Van Gundy's leadership, New York returned to a winning style, featuring strong rebounding and defense. The focus on a tenacious defense became evident in the team's playoff run to the NBA Finals with Van Gundy in 1999.

A Modest Record

The Knicks had finished the lockout-shortened 1998–99 regular season with a 27–23 mark. They had struggled all year, nearly missing the playoffs. Their record ended up being good enough for fourth place in the Atlantic Division, and the eighth and final spot in the Eastern Conference playoff picture. What happened during the playoff run was amazing.

Making History

In the first round, New York beat the Miami Heat in five games, three games to two. The Heat, coached by former Knicks head coach Pat Riley, played a very physical series against New York.

The fifth and deciding game went right down to the last second. Knicks guard Allan Houston's floating shot bounced into the net with just a second left in the game, giving New York a first-round victory.

In the Eastern Conference semifinals, the Knicks faced the Atlanta Hawks. Amazingly, New York had little trouble with the Hawks, beating them in four straight games.

In the 1999 Eastern Conference Finals, the Knicks faced the Indiana Pacers, a team that many thought would win the NBA championship. New York had other ideas.

A Star Falls, a New Star Is Born

In Game 2, star center Patrick Ewing tore his Achilles tendon, ending his season. During the regular season Ewing had led the team in scoring and rebounding. He would be tough to replace. Marcus Camby stepped up his game and became the Knicks new "ready-for-prime-time" player.

Camby got more playing time, and his statistics increased as well. During the regular season, Camby had averaged 7.2 points, 5.5 rebounds, and 1.6 blocks

M *arcus Camby joined the Knicks prior to the 1998–99 season in a trade that sent Charles Oakley to the Toronto Raptors.*

pcr game. In the final four contests of the Pacers series, Camby averaged 18.8 points, 11.8 rebounds, and 3.3 blocks per game.

Following the series, Pacers head coach Larry Bird said that Camby was "the MVP of the series."[1]

"I knew I just needed my opportunity," added Camby. "The playoffs provided it."[2]

The Turning Point

The game that many Knicks fans will remember from that series was Game 3. With both teams exchanging the lead during the game, the contest came down to the final seconds. With time running out and the game on the line, New York's Larry Johnson was fouled as he made a three-pointer. He added the foul shot, making it a four-point play—a rare occurrence. That point not only gave the Knicks a one-point victory over the Pacers, but it was a turning point in the series.

With Camby, Houston, and Latrell Sprewell leading the way, the Knicks became an athletically dynamic team that defeated the Pacers in six games. Houston, who was a hero for New York against Miami, came through again in Game 6 against Indiana, scoring 32 points. The Knicks became the first eighth-seeded team to reach the NBA Finals.

Final Showdown

In the finals, the Knicks faced the Western Conference champion San Antonio Spurs. The Spurs had lost only one game in the first three rounds of the playoffs.

The New York Knicks Basketball Team

*L*arry Bird looks on as Larry Johnson shoots a three-pointer over Antonio Davis. Johnson made the shot and was fouled. He made the foul shot for a rarely seen four-point play.

Unfortunately for the Knicks, injuries caught up with them. In addition to Ewing being out, Johnson suffered a sprained knee in Game 6 of the Pacers series. The Spurs proved too much for the Knicks. San Antonio defeated New York in five games to win the NBA championship.

For the Knicks it was the end of a magic ride. Van Gundy may have summed it up best. He said, "The question we have to answer is: Was the playoffs catching lightning in a bottle and a bit of a mirage, or can the way it ended be our reality?"[3]

Only time will tell for the Knicks.

STATISTICS

Team Record

The Knicks History

YEARS	LOCATION	W	L	PCT	CHAMPIONSHIPS
1946–47 to 1949–50	New York	131	105	.555	None
1950–51 to 1959–60	New York	375	334	.529	Eastern Division, 1951–54*
1960–61 to 1969–70	New York	347	459	.431	Eastern Division, 1970 NBA Champs, 1970
1970–71 to 1979–80	New York	437	383	.533	Atlantic Division, 1971 Eastern Conference, 1972–73 NBA Champs, 1973
1980–81 to 1989–90	New York	380	440	.463	Atlantic Division, 1989
1990–91 to 1998–99	New York	436	270	.618	Atlantic Division, 1992–94 Eastern Conference, 1994 Eastern Conference, 1999

*New York won the Eastern Division playoffs in 1951–53. In 1954, the Knicks were regular season division champs, but lost in the Divisional playoffs.

The Knicks Today

SEASON	SEASON RECORD	PLAYOFF RECORD	HEAD COACH	DIVISION FINISH
1990–91	39–43	0–3	Stu Jackson John MacLeod	3rd
1991–92	51–31	6–6	Pat Riley	1st (tie)
1992–93	60–22	9–6	Pat Riley	1st
1993–94	57–25	14–11	Pat Riley	1st

The New York Knicks Basketball Team

The Knicks Today (continued)

SEASON	SEASON RECORD	PLAYOFF RECORD	HEAD COACH	DIVISION FINISH
1994–95	55–27	6–5	Pat Riley	2nd
1995–96	47–35	4–4	Don Nelson Jeff Van Gundy	2nd
1996–97	57–25	6–4	Jeff Van Gundy	2nd
1997–98	43–39	4–6	Jeff Van Gundy	2nd
1998–99	27–23	12–8	Jeff Van Gundy	4th

Total History

SEASON RECORD	PLAYOFF RECORD	NBA CHAMPIONSHIPS
2,106–1,991	168–161	2

Coaching Records

COACH	YEARS COACHED	RECORD	CHAMPIONSHIPS
Neil Cohalan	1946–47	33–27	None
Joe Lapchick	1947–56	326–247	Eastern Division, 1951–54
Vince Boryla	1956–58	80–85	None
Fuzzy Levane	1958–59	48–51	None
Carl Braun	1959–61	40–87	None
Eddie Donovan	1961–65	84–194	None
Harry Gallatin	1965	25–38	None
Dick McGuire	1965–67	75–102	None
Red Holzman	1967–77 1978–82	613–484	NBA Champions, 1970, 1973 Eastern Division, 1970 Eastern Conference, 1972–73 Atlantic Division, 1971
Willis Reed	1977–78	49–47	None

Coaching Records (continued)

COACH	YEARS COACHED	RECORD	CHAMPIONSHIPS
Hubie Brown	1982–86	142–202	None
Bob Hill	1986–87	20–46	None
Rick Pitino	1987–89	90–74	Atlantic Division, 1989
Stu Jackson	1989–90	52–45	None
John MacLeod	1990–91	32–35	None
Pat Riley	1991–95	223–105	Eastern Conference, 1994 Atlantic Division, 1992–94
Don Nelson	1995–96	34–25	None
Jeff Van Gundy	1996–99	140–97	Eastern Conference, 1999

Ten Great Knicks

PLAYER	SEA	YRS	G	REB	AST	STL	BLK	PTS	AVG
Bill Bradley[H]	1967–77	10	742	2,354	2,533	209*	65*	9,217	12.4
Dave DeBusschere[H]	1968–74	12	875	9,618	2,497	67*	39*	14,053	16.1
Patrick Ewing	1985–99	14	977	10,155	2,030	1,025	2,674	22,736	23.3
Walt Frazier[H]	1967–77	13	825	4,830	5,040	681*	59*	15,581	18.9
Harry Gallatin[H]	1948–57	10	682	6,684*	1,208	—	—	8,843	13.0
Allan Houston	1996–99	6	450	1,253	1,042	295	94	6,905	15.3
Bernard King	1982–87**	14	874	5,060	2,863	866	230	19,655	22.5
Earl Monroe[H]	1971–80	13	926	2,796	3,594	473*	121*	17,454	18.8
Charles Oakley	1988–98	14	1,018	10,469	2,544	1,111	274	10,822	10.6
Willis Reed[H]	1964–74	10	650	8,414	1,186	12*	21*	12,183	18.7

SEA=Seasons with Knicks   YRS=Years in the NBA   G=Games
REB=Rebounds   AST=Assists   STL=Steals
BLK=Blocks   PTS=Points   AVG=Points per game

*Statistics are incomplete for some players in some categories. The NBA did not keep statistics for rebounds until the 1950–51 season, and for steals and blocked shots until the 1973–74 season.
**Bernard King was on the Knicks roster from 1982–87, but he missed the entire 1985–86 season due to injury.
[H]Member of Naismith Memorial Basketball Hall of Fame

The New York Knicks Basketball Team

CHAPTER NOTES

Chapter 1. Greatest Moment
1. Tim Crothers, *Sports Illustrated: Greatest Teams* (Alexandria, Va.: Time-Life, Inc., 1998), p. 140.

2. Taken from NBA Video: *NBA at 50: Golden Anniversary Collector's Edition*. Produced by NBA Entertainment, 1997. Distributed by Library Video Company, Wynnewood, Pa.

3. Ibid.

4. Ibid.

5. Ibid.

6. Ibid.

Chapter 2. History of the Knicks
1. Taken from NBA Video: *NBA at 50: Golden Anniversary Collector's Edition*. Produced by NBA Entertainment, 1997. Distributed by Library Video Company, Wynnewood, Pa.

2. George Kalinsky, *The New York Knicks: The Official 50th Anniversary Celebration* (Old Tappan, N.J.: Macmillan, 1996), p. 30.

Chapter 3. Greatest Knicks Players
1. Mark Vancil, ed., *NBA at 50* (New York: Park Lane Press, 1996), p. 88.

2. Ibid., p. 109.

3. Ibid., p. 89.

4. Ibid., p. 97.

Chapter 4. Greatest Knicks Coaches
1. George Kalinsky, *The New York Knicks: The Official 50th Anniversary Celebration* (Old Tappan, N.J.: Macmillan, 1996), p. 16.

2. Ibid., p. 110.

Chapter 5. Greatest Knicks Seasons
1. George Kalinsky, *The New York Knicks: The Official 50th Anniversary Celebration* (Old Tappan, N.J.: Macmillan, 1996), p. 124.

2. Ibid., p. 194.

Chapter 6. Cinderella Season
1. Jeff Ryan, "Atlantic Division," *Sporting News 1999–2000 Pro Basketball Magazine* (Times Mirror, St. Louis: Mo., 1999), p. 12.

2. Ibid.

3. Greg Logan, "New York Knicks," *Sporting News 1999–2000 Pro Basketball Magazine* (Times Mirror, St. Louis: Mo., 1999), p. 23.

GLOSSARY

ABA—American Basketball Association. This group of teams was formed in 1967 and was created as an alternative to the National Basketball Association (NBA). It lasted nine seasons before merging with the NBA.

assist—A successful pass to a teammate that results in a basket for the team.

blocked shot—This occurs when a defensive player gets his hand on a shot taken by an offensive player.

center—Often the tallest player on the court. His job is to block shots, grab rebounds, and make easy shots near the basket.

draft—The selection of amateur players, in a rotating order, each year by NBA teams. The team with the worst record generally picks first.

forwards—The players on a basketball team whose positions are on either side of the center along the end of the court. Forwards are usually among the taller players.

foul—Illegal physical contact against an opposing player.

general manager—The official in charge of building the team by getting players, either through the draft, by trades, or by signing free agents. The general manager is in charge of those aspects of the team not overseen by the coaching staff.

give-and-go—A play in basketball in which a player passes the ball to a teammate, cuts to the basket, and gets a pass from the teammate he just passed to.

guards—The players on a basketball team whose positions are more toward the midcourt line than the two forwards and the center. Guards are usually the shortest players on the team but are the best ball-handlers and shooters.

jump shot—The player jumps, usually to get space over a defender, brings the ball up into shooting position, and fires at the basket.

key—The area that includes the free-throw lane and the semicircle behind the free-throw line.

lottery—The system in the player draft by which teams not making the playoffs draw to determine the drafting order. The lottery was created to prevent teams from deliberately losing games to get the number-one draft choice.

NBA—National Basketball Association. The NBA formed in 1947 after the merger of the Basketball Association of America (BAA) and the National Basketball League (NBL). The Knicks were one of the NBA's original franchises.

NIT—National Invitational Tournament. The NIT invites college basketball teams that did not reach the prestigious NCAA Tournament.

overtime—The additional period or periods called for if a game is tied at the end of regulation play. Regulation periods are twelve minutes each; overtime periods are five minutes.

pivot—The area near the basket.

rebound—A ball grabbed after a missed shot bounces off the rim or backboard.

steal—This occurs when one player is able to take the ball away from the opposing team.

three-point shot—A field goal that is worth three points. The shot is taken from beyond the three-point line, which has ranged from 22 feet to 23 feet, 9 inches from the basket.

FURTHER READING

Berger, Phil. *The Miracle on 33rd Street: The New York Knickerbockers' Championship Season, 1969–70*. New York: Four Walls Eight Windows, 1994.

Bradley, Bill. *Life on the Run*. New York: Vintage Books, 1995.

Goodman, Michael. *New York Knicks*. Mankato, Minn.: The Creative Company, 1993.

Holzman, Red, and Leonard Levin. *My Unforgettable Season, 1970*. New York: Tor Books, 1994.

Joseph, Paul. *The New York Knicks*. Edina, Minn.: ABDO Publishing Company, 1997.

Kalinsky, George. *The New York Knicks: The Official 50th Anniversary Celebration*. Old Tappan, N.J.: Macmillan Publishing Company, 1996.

Kavanagh, Jack. *Sports Great Patrick Ewing*. Hillside, N.J.: Enslow Publishers, Inc., 1992.

Knapp, Ron. *Top 10 Basketball Centers*. Hillside, N.J.: Enslow Publishers, Inc., 1994.

Lee, Spike, and Ralph Wiley. *The Best Seat in the House: A Basketball Memoir*. New York: Crown Publishing Group, 1998.

Mekz, Andrew K. *Knicks Grit: Words of Wisdom from the Brash, Bold, Big Hearted 1994 New York Knicks*. Swarthmore, Pa.: Wit Press, 1994.

Reiser, Howard. *Patrick Ewing: Center of Attention*. Danbury, Conn.: Children's Press, 1994.

The New York Knicks Basketball Team

INDEX

WHERE TO WRITE

The New York Knicks
Madison Square Garden
2 Penn Plaza, 14th Floor
New York, NY 10121

WEB SITES

http://www.nba.com/knicks
http://espn.go.com/nba/clubhouses/nyk.html